NICK JR. BLUE'S ROOM

It's Hug Day!

adapted by Sarah Willson

based on the teleplay by Angela C. Santomero

Simon Spotlight/Nick Jr.

New York   London   Toronto   Sydney

Based on the TV series *Blue's Clues*® created by Traci Paige Johnson,
Todd Kessler, and Angela C. Santomero as seen on Nick Jr.®
Photos by Joan Marcus and Ken Karp Photography.
Some illustrations on pages 3, 4, 8, 14, 15, 17, 18, 19, 21, 22, 23, and 24 by Karen Craig.

3 1350 00256 7685

SIMON SPOTLIGHT
An imprint of Simon & Schuster Children's Publishing Division
1230 Avenue of the Americas, New York, New York 10020
© 2006 Viacom International Inc. All rights reserved.
NICK JR., *Blue's Clues*, *Blue's Room*, and all related titles, logos, and characters are
trademarks of Viacom International Inc. Created by Traci Paige Johnson, Todd Kessler, and Angela C. Santomero.
All rights reserved, including the right of reproduction in whole or in part in any form.
SIMON SPOTLIGHT and colophon are registered trademarks of Simon & Schuster, Inc.
Manufactured in the United States of America
10 9 8 7 6 5 4 3
ISBN-13: 978-1-4169-0222-5
ISBN-10: 1-4169-0222-8

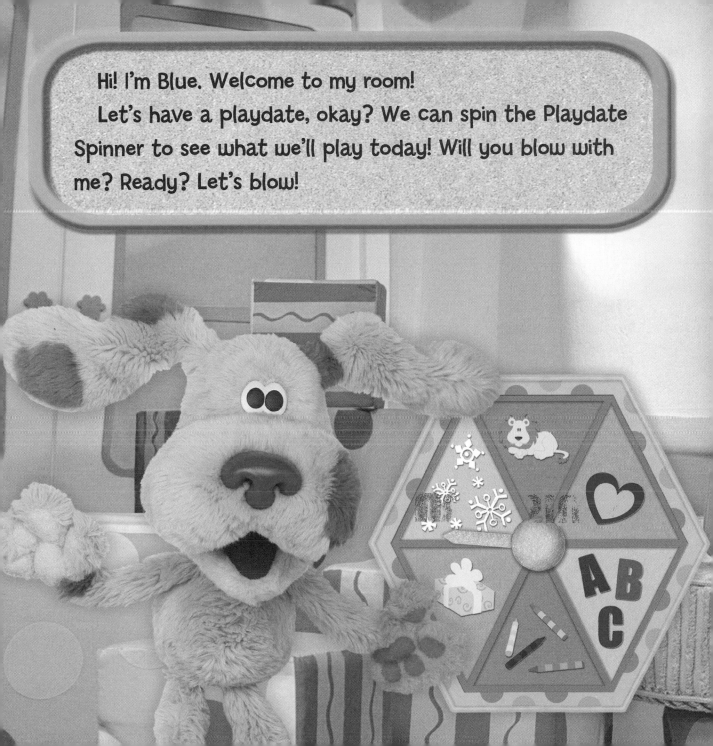

The Playdate Spinner landed on Hug Day. Hooray! What do you think we do on a Hug Day Playdate? Yeah, we give hugs to everyone we love. Whoa, nice hug, Roar E.! Thanks!

Hi, Polka Dots!

Ooooooh! Polka Dots has a special Hug Day Polka Dots Puzzle Surprise for us. And here's the first puzzle piece! Look! It's a picture of three crayons. I wonder what we're going to make.

Awww, nice hug, Fred! You're giving me a hug because you *appreciate* me? That's so cool!

. . . DICTIONARY!

Hmmm . . . let's see. Dictionary says that "appreciate" means to love, enjoy, and want to hug.

Appreciate!

Oooh! I *appreciate* you, Polka Dots, because you're my friend. So I'm going to give you a hug!

How about you? Hug someone *you* appreciate!

Hmmm. It's a picture of some glue. I wonder what our surprise will be.

It's a teacher! We appreciate how teachers help us learn things—like saying the alphabet and tying our shoes. Who else do *you* appreciate?

Look! Doodleboard is going to doodle another picture of something we appreciate. But what will it be?

There's Polka Dots again. And he has our last puzzle piece.

Look at that. It's a picture of some construction paper.

Now let's put our puzzle together.
It's a . . .